CATCHER WITH A GLASS ARM

THE #1
SPORTS SERIES
FOR KIDS

CATCHER WITH A
GLASS ARM

LITTLE, BROWN AND COMPANY
New York Boston

Little, Brown and Company

Hachette Book Group
1290 Avenue of the Americas, New York, NY 10104
Visit us at lb-kids.com

mattchristopher.com

Little, Brown and Company is a division of Hachette Book Group, Inc.
The Little, Brown name and logo are trademarks of Hachette Book Group, Inc.

The publisher is not responsible for websites (or their content) that are not owned by the publisher.

First Paperback Edition: May 1985
First published in hardcover in January 1964 by Little, Brown and Company

Matt Christopher® is a registered trademark of Matt Christopher Royalties, Inc.

ISBN 978-0-316-13985-4

Library of Congress Control Number 64-10169

40 39 38 37 36

LSC-C

Printed in the United States of America

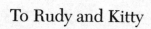

To Rudy and Kitty

CATCHER WITH A GLASS ARM

Ball two!"

Jody had to reach almost out of the catcher's box for that pitch. He looked at the runner on first. The Tigers' man was jumping back and forth, teasing Jody to throw the ball.

Jody didn't know what to do. If he threw to second base, he might throw wild. He had a poor peg. If he threw to first, the runner might dash for second.

"Throw it here!" yelled Moonie Myers angrily.

Jody tossed the ball to Moonie, who was

waiting for it about six feet in front of the pitcher's mound. That settled his problem for a while.

Moonie toed the rubber, looked at the man on first, then pitched.

"Strike two!"

That pitch breezed in knee-high, about an inch from the outside corner. Jody caught it smack in the pocket of his mitt. It stung a little.

Then Jody saw the runner on first take off like a shot for second base. Sweat broke out on his face. Even before he threw he knew that the ball would not reach second. He could catch any pitch near the plate, but he could not throw a ball within twenty feet of a target.

Jody saw Rabbit Foote run from his shortstop position to cover the bag. Jody heaved the ball. It arced over Moonie's head like a fat balloon and struck the grass short and to the left of Rabbit.

Rabbit caught the hop. By the time he tried to make the play, the runner was already on the base.

The Tigers' bench let out a lusty cheer. They had plenty to cheer about, too. This was the last of the fourth inning, and they were leading 5–4. Now there was a man on second and no outs. They had a good chance to fatten that score.

Rabbit tossed the ball to a disgusted Moonie Myers and trotted back to his position. He was small but quick-footed as the animal for which he was nicknamed. He had a lot of spark, too. He showed it now as he started a chatter that spread like wildfire among the other infielders.

Jody joined in, but it was hard to yell through an aching throat. It was his fault that a man was on second base, just as it was his fault that the Tigers had got two runs in the second inning. At that time he had thrown wild again to second, and two men had scored. He had expected Coach Jack Fisher to put in somebody else to catch. But there was no other catcher.

Moonie breezed in the next pitch. *Whiff!* One out.

The next hitter flied out to left field. Then Jody caught a high pop fly, and the inning was over.

Jody breathed a sigh of relief. He took off his catching gear, put on a protective helmet, and picked up a bat. He was leading off this inning. Boy, he'd like to hit that ball this time. A hit would make up for that bad throw to second.

"Batter up!" cried the umpire.

Jody stepped to the plate. He was a left-handed hitter, already with a single and a walk to his credit. He let the first pitch go by, then swung at the next. The bat connected with the ball solidly. The white pill flashed over second, and Jody rounded first for a clean double.

The fans cheered, and the knot that had lodged in Jody's stomach disappeared. That was what a good hit did for you. It was like medicine. It made you feel all well again.

Right fielder Roddie Nelson let a pitch go by that was straight down the heart of the plate.

Another pitch breezed in, curving across the outside corner. Roddie swung. Missed!

Jody, leading off the bag, turned and trotted back. He tried to remember when Roddie had got his last hit. He just couldn't. This was their second league game, and Roddie had not yet touched first base. Roddie was just hopeless, that's all.

The pitch. "Ball one!" Roddie almost swung at that one.

The pitch again. It looked good. Roddie swung. *Crack!* It was a beautiful sound. Real solid. Jody saw the ball flash like a meteor over his head, and he knew it carried a label on it. A home-run label.

The ball sailed over the left-field fence for Roddie's first hit of the year — a two-run homer.

The fans had never cheered so loudly. Roddie came in, crossing the plate behind Jody. He was so happy he couldn't say a word. Jody was the first to shake his hand and congratulate him.

"Nice socko, Roddie!"

There were no more hits that inning. Now the score was 6–5 in the Dolphins' favor.

Moonie worked hard on the first batter and struck him out. Then a single through short changed things quickly. The runner was the Tigers' lead-off man, a speedster on the base paths.

He took a small lead as Moonie climbed upon the mound.

"Steal, Peter!" a Tigers player yelled from the bench. "That catcher can't throw! He's got a glass arm!"

Jody winced. *A glass arm.* Nobody had ever said that about him before.

2

Moonie stretched, looked at the man on first. Quickly he turned and snapped the ball to first baseman Birdie Davis. The runner scooted back safely.

Birdie returned the ball to Moonie. Once again Moonie went through his stretch. Again came the cry from the Tigers' bench:

"Steal, Peter!"

The pitch came in, slightly high and outside. Jody caught it. He saw the runner racing for second, head lowered and arms pumping hard. Jody heaved the ball, making sure he didn't throw too hard for fear the ball might sail over Rabbit Foote's head.

Instead — the ball fell short! Rabbit missed the hop and the ball bounced out to the outfield. The runner raced on, to third. He stayed there as center fielder Arnie Smith made a perfect peg in to Moonie.

"I told you he had a glass arm, Peter!" yelled that same voice from the Tigers' bench.

Jody tried to ignore the cry. But he couldn't. The words *glass arm* stormed through his mind like an echo.

Moonie toed the rubber and threw in a low inside pitch that was probably harder than any he had thrown. Jody never thought that the batter would bite at it. But the batter did. He hit a dribbler toward the mound. Moonie picked it up and tossed it to first for the put-out.

Two outs. The runner was still on third.

One more out, thought Jody . . . just one more, and this rough inning will be over.

Crack! A line drive over Moonie's head! The runner scored, and the hitter held up at first.

The game was tied up now, 6–6. Jody pressed his lips firmly together, yanked on his chest protector, and returned to his spot behind the plate.

The pitch . . . a hit to short! Rabbit picked it up, threw to second. . . . *Out!*

Jody whipped off his mask and walked to the bench. He didn't look at anyone, but he heard someone from behind the backstop screen say, "Don't let it bother you, Jody. You'll get that ball up there."

On the bench Coach Jack Fisher patted Jody on the knee. "You seem to be afraid to throw that ball, pal. Heave it hard. Let it fly."

Jody shook his head. There was nothing he could say.

Now Mike Brink, pinch-hitting for Arnie Smith, started the ball rolling. He singled through second, and scored on a double by Johnny Bartho. That was all the Dolphins put across that half-inning, but it was enough. The Tigers couldn't do a thing at their turn at bat, and the game went to the Dolphins, 7–6.

Jody removed his catching gear and put it into the canvas bag. He had started walking toward the gate when a tall, thin man with a crew cut and dark-rimmed glasses approached him.

"Good game, Jody. You did a great job behind that plate."

"Thank you," said Jody, trying to smile. "Guess I can't throw worth beans, though."

"Don't worry. You have a strong arm. I can tell. You're just afraid to use all that power." He smiled and Jody smiled with him.

"Want to come home with us?" the man invited.

Jody didn't know whom he meant by "us." He had never seen the man before. "No, thanks," he said. "I don't live very far from here. I can walk home."

"Okay. See you at the next game."

"Good-bye," said Jody.

The man walked toward Coach Fisher and a group of boys who were helping him load up the canvas bag. Jody turned and stepped through the gate.

"Meowrrrr!"

Jody grinned. "Hi, Midnight," he greeted. "Come to meet me, did you?"

The black cat rubbed up against Jody's leg, and Jody bent down to pet it. Midnight was really a wonderful pet. He tagged after Jody almost everywhere Jody went. And Jody loved him. He probably loved Midnight as much as he did baseball.

He found Rabbit and Birdie waiting for him too, and they all walked home together.

Rabbit talked a blue streak most of the time, hardly giving Birdie or Jody a chance to squeeze in a word. But that was Rabbit for you. Jody liked him a lot.

Then Rabbit said, "Gets me why you can't throw that ball to second, Jody. Boy! Would I like to have tagged that one kid. He runs like a streak, but we'd have had him if you'd thrown the ball at the bag."

"I know," admitted Jody. "But I can't. That's all there is to it. I just can't."

He suddenly remembered what a Tigers player had said — glass arm.

"Moonie was real sore," said Birdie. "Maybe he won't pitch any more."

Jody's mouth dropped. "Why not?"

Birdie shrugged. "Oh. You know how he is."

Jody pressed his lips together. Yes, he knew how Moonie was. But it was *him* Moonie was sore at.

3

The sun was blazing overhead just before noon Saturday as the blue car zipped along Route 4. In the front seat were Mom and Dad Sinclair. In back were Jody, his sister, Diane, Rabbit Foote, and, of course, Midnight. They were going on a picnic.

It wasn't going to be just an ordinary picnic, though. Dad had plans. As a matter of fact, it was his idea to have Rabbit come along.

Jody didn't know what those plans could be. Dad had suggested that they bring along a bat, baseball, and some baseball gloves.

That was strange since Dad, a real golf bug, had his bag of clubs in the trunk with the food.

Lincoln Park was thirteen miles away from home. It was a beautiful green spot with hills protecting it on all sides. There were picnic tables sheltered underneath trees and along the hillsides. There was a large swimming pool already dotted with swimmers. There was a softball diamond, and plenty of room to drive a baseball a mile.

There were already golfers practicing on long and short putts. That was what Dad liked to do, too.

Dad parked the car. Jody and Rabbit found a vacant table nearby.

Dad asked, "Do you kids want to go swimming until lunch is ready?"

"Okay by me," said Rabbit.

The boys ran to the bathhouse with their trunks. At their heels raced Midnight, his black tail high in the air. The boys got into their trunks and then dived off a low diving board into the cool, clean pool.

It was almost half an hour later when Diane came after them. From the edge of the pool she cupped her hands to her mouth and shouted:

"Jody! Rabbit! Come and get i-i-i-it! You, too, Midnight!" she added.

The boys climbed out of the pool and walked to the picnic table, water dripping off their bodies. Diane tossed each a towel, and they dried themselves as best as they could. Then they sat and ate. After that they were too full to swim anymore. Anyway, they knew they shouldn't so soon after eating. They went to the bathhouse and dressed.

"Bet Dad will be out there with his golf clubs," said Jody as they started out the door.

"He's out there, but not with his golf clubs," observed Rabbit. "He has the bat, ball, and gloves. Guess he wants to give us a workout, Jody."

"We're going to have some throwing practice," said Dad. "Rabbit, take this glove and get down there about where second base would be. Jody, put on your mitt. I'll get halfway between, about where the pitcher's box would be. I want to see you throw that ball, Jody. In those games I've seen I can tell that you're holding back. You're not throwing that ball at all as you should."

So that was it, thought Jody. *And I never even thought he cared how I threw!*

Dad laid the bat aside and threw the baseball to Jody. "Okay. Throw it back to me," he said.

Jody threw it easily. Too easily. It struck the ground two feet in front of his father.

"Throw them up here, Jody!" said Dad, holding his glove against his chest.

Jody tried again. Still low.

"You're straining too hard, Jody," said Dad. "Snap your wrist. Like this."

Jody watch his dad move his wrist back and forth as if it worked on a hinge. Then he tried to do the same thing. He succeeded, and a pleased smile came to his lips.

He threw the ball to his dad. It floated through the air like a balloon.

"Why are you afraid to throw that ball?" cried Dad. "Why?" He was almost angry.

Jody shrugged. "I don't know." He really didn't. He *wanted* to throw the ball hard. He *wanted* to snap it as his dad did. But he couldn't.

"All right," said Dad. "Throw it to second."

Jody reared back and pegged the ball over his dad's head. It hit the ground and bounced twice before it reached Rabbit.

Dad didn't like that at all. He shook his head from side to side.

"Try it again, Jody. Keep your feet straight and don't move them. Bring that ball back over your shoulder and then snap it like a whip."

Jody tried it. He threw the ball fairly straight, but it was low. It went directly at Dad, and he caught it.

"That's the idea," said Dad. "But aim at Rabbit."

Jody aimed at Rabbit, but Rabbit wasn't where he threw the ball. Dad had him try again and again, making Jody practice short throws to him and long throws to Rabbit. Once in a while Jody threw the ball exactly where he was supposed to. But most of the time he didn't.

"Oh, Jody!" cried Dad finally. "*How* can I teach you? I *know* you can throw a ball harder than that."

Dad's face was red. You could tell he was angry. He was sweating, too. They had been out here at least an hour.

"Put the stuff back into the car," Dad said. "We'll have to leave soon, anyway. There's a storm coming."

He walked with giant strides across the park, leaving the boys to gather the bat, ball, and gloves. Jody watched his back. A lump formed in his throat and stuck there. *He's disappointed in me. But what can I do? I've tried as hard as I can.*

A wind came up suddenly. It whipped the tops of trees and shook leaves loose from their branches. Everything and everybody were in the car when the first big drops of rain splashed against the windshield. Midnight huddled like a black ball on Jody's lap, purring. Dad started the car and drove it hurriedly out of the park.

The rain fell thicker and harder. Black clouds swirled and twisted in the sky. Forks of lightning pierced the clouds.

Dad slowed the speed of the car. The windshield wipers were whipping back and forth, but the rain came down so hard that the wipers were hardly doing any good.

"I'll park off the road as soon as I find a place," said Dad. "This is certainly bad, but it won't last."

Suddenly a great blinding flash lit up the half-darkened sky. Everything seemed to turn white for one instant. Then a terrible sound filled the air.

Just ahead of them Jody saw a tree break in the middle and collapse across the road!

"Dad! Watch it!" he screamed, and hugged Midnight tightly against him.

From the rear seat Mom and Diane let

out frightened cries. Dad shoved in the brake pedal. The car swerved, then stopped. Luckily he was driving slowly. But Jody heard a *bump* beside him. He turned and stared at Rabbit lying with his head back against the seat. His eyes were closed, and a red welt stuck out on his forehead!

"Rabbit!" Jody cried, and shook his friend by the arm. "Rabbit!"

Rabbit didn't move.

Jody turned wide, horrified eyes at his Dad.

"Dad," he whispered, "is he dead?"

4

Dad leaned across Jody's lap. He lifted Rabbit's head.

"Rabbit!" he said, rubbing the boy's cheeks with his hands. "Wake up, son."

Rabbit's eyes blinked open. He moaned and lifted a hand to the bump on his forehead.

Jody took a deep breath and smiled with relief. "Boy! You had me scared!"

"Sorry, Rabbit," said Dad. "You smacked your head against the window when I swerved. I'll wet my handkerchief. You can hold it against the bruise to help stop the pain."

He opened the window on his side and held out his handkerchief in the rain. When it was real wet, he squeezed most of the water out of it, folded it several times, and put it against the bruise on Rabbit's head.

"There you are," said Dad. "Now just hold it there awhile."

Jody looked at his friend with an ache in his heart. That was only a bump, but Rabbit's face looked very pale. He didn't look well at all.

"Are we in a pickle!" murmured Dad.

Jody looked at him, then looked outside. Tree limbs were hanging over the roof of the car, and the tree trunk was blocking their path in front of them.

"Guess we're stuck," said Jody.

"Thank God we didn't get hit by that

tree," said Mom. "Looks as if we'll just have to sit here until the rain stops and somebody removes it."

"Your deduction is quite correct, Martha," replied Dad.

The black clouds twisted and spiraled away, and the rain stopped almost as quickly as it had begun.

"I'm going out a minute," said Rabbit, and opened the door.

"Rabbit!" Dad shouted. "No! Close that door and keep it closed!"

Rabbit slammed the door and turned a white face and wide, terrified eyes to Jody's father.

"I'm sorry, Mr. Sinclair," murmured Rabbit. "I almost forgot. That tree could have pulled down some wires. Dangerous wires."

Dad looked seriously at Rabbit. "That's right, Rabbit. By stepping outside you could have really injured yourself."

"I know," said Rabbit. "I just wasn't thinking, I guess."

A few minutes later a car came alongside
them and stopped. It was the first car they
had seen since the tree had been struck. A
man and woman were in the car.

"Has anybody gone to get help for you?"
yelled the man.

"No," replied Dad. "We'll be very much
obliged if you'll report this to the police, sir."

"We'll do that," said the man, and drove
off.

In less than ten minutes, a large truck
with tools and equipment piled on it drove
up. Four men got out. One was carrying a
chain saw. Another approached Dad.

"Everybody all right, sir?" he asked.

"Quite all right, except for one young pas-
senger," said Dad. "He banged his head
against the window when I hit the brakes."

The man shook his head. "Sorry to hear

that, but it could've been worse. That tree pulled down a few wires with it. The lines are dead now. You can move on once there's room."

"Thank you very much," said Dad.

The four men went to work on the tree and before too long had cleared a path. Dad drove away, waving back to them.

"Well," said Mom, "that was an experience I'll never forget as long as I live."

"Me, too," said Diane.

Jody didn't say anything. He was thinking about Rabbit. How badly was he hurt? Would he be able to play in Wednesday's game? Without Rabbit playing shortstop, the team would hardly have a chance against the Gophers. And if Rabbit didn't play, the whole team would blame Jody.

I wish it was me who got hurt — not Rabbit, thought Jody.

When the game rolled around Wednesday evening against the Gophers, Rabbit Foote was not in the lineup. His head was still swollen. The doctor had said that he had better not play baseball for a week at least.

Jody was nearly sick all day thinking about it. He blamed Dad a little, too, at first. But then, it wasn't Dad's fault that a storm had come up and a bolt of lightning had struck the tree and knocked it down. That was an accident.

Dad was really sorry that Rabbit had got hurt. He seemed to feel as responsible as Jody did.

After the teams had their batting and in-field practices, the Gophers took the field.

The Dolphins started well that first in-ning. With two away, Arnie Smith singled and Johnny Bartho singled. But the Go-phers snuffed out the Dolphins' chance of scoring by catching Joe Bell's grounder and throwing him out. Joe was playing short in place of Rabbit.

The Gophers came to bat and scored a run. In the second inning the Dolphins picked up two.

Nothing serious happened again until the bottom of the third. The Gophers got hot. With one man out, they began to pow-der Moonie's pitches as if it were batting-practice time. To make matters worse, Jody threw twice to third, in an effort to nab a runner, and both times the ball hit the ground far in front of third baseman Duane West. Duane and Moonie yelled their heads off at him. Jody could even hear Dad shouting from the bleachers.

"Come on, Jody! Throw the ball *up!*"

But all the yelling in the world would not have done any good. Nobody knew that but Jody.

When, finally, the inning ended, the Gophers had put across four runs. Moonie came in shaking his head. He had his lips clamped together, and his eyes didn't lift once to the players around him. You could tell that he was taking most of the blame.

Moonie hated errors or bad plays, no matter who made them. Jody wished Moonie wouldn't be like that. Baseball wasn't much fun with a guy who acted that way on the team, no matter if he did pitch a good game most of the time.

It was Moonie himself who started things off with a bang in the top of the fourth. He socked a triple against the left-field fence, and then scored on Duane's single. Frank York flied out. Arnie put life back into the team by knocking out a double. Left fielder Johnny Bartho, who was Moonie's best pal, singled. Joe Bell, after hitting four fouls, finally banged out a single, too.

Hunk Peters, the tall right-hander for the Gophers, must have become tired throwing all those pitches. He walked Birdie Davis on four straight balls. You would think that the coach would send Hunk to the showers, but he didn't

Then Jody grounded out, and Roddie struck out, and the big inning was over. Score: Dolphins 6; Gophers 5.

The Gophers didn't lose heart. With two outs, they began to hit again. Moonie looked as if the world were going to collapse on his shoulders. He yelled at Jody for not throwing the ball high enough to second, when a runner stole. He yelled at Joe Bell for throwing wild to home. He kicked the rubber when the batters knocked out base hits.

And then Coach Fisher climbed out of the dugout, called "Time!" and walked out to the mound. Jody stood behind the plate, waiting.

The coach put an arm around Moonie's shoulders and talked to him. The pitcher looked up at him and then looked away again, shaking his head unhappily. The coach kept talking to him. Then a smile appeared on Moonie's face. When the coach walked off the field, the fans cheered, and even Jody smiled.

Moonie didn't yell any more. Nor did the Gophers get any more hits. But they had already scored two runs, putting them one ahead of the Dolphins.

Moonie led off in the fifth inning. He received a big hand as he stepped to the plate. Hunk walked him, and then struck out Duane.

Mike Brink pinch-hit for Frank, and singled through the pitcher's box. Moonie went to second. Arnie walked, Johnny Bartho struck out, and Joe Bell came through with another single that scored Moonie.

It was Joe's third hit of the game. The crowd gave him a tremendous cheer, because Joe was usually poor at the plate as well as in the field.

"How do you like that?" said Coach Fisher, grinning broadly. "That boy's playing like a big leaguer today."

Birdie flied out, ending the inning.

The score was tied, 7-all. But again the Gophers came through, scoring to break the tie.

Jody led off in the top of the sixth. This was the Dolphins' last chance.

Jody tapped the tip of the bat against the plate and waited for the pitch he wanted.

"Strike!" The ball just grazed the inside corner.

Another pitch. Jody stepped toward it, lifting his bat.

No. Too high! "Ball!"

Hunk scraped some dirt into the hole in front of the rubber. Then he stepped on the rubber and made his windup.

He breezed the ball in. It sailed toward the plate like a white streak — a little high, and inside. Jody stepped into it again. Just as it approached the plate, the ball curved in. Jody tried to duck.

Smack! The ball struck the front right side

of his helmet, glanced off, and Jody fell. With the helmet on, he hardly felt any pain. But stars blinked like lightning bugs in front of his eyes.

He heard feet pounding on the ground. And then a voice crying, "Oh, no!"

6

Jody sat there awhile, his eyes closed.

Someone yanked off his helmet and put a cool hand against his head.

"I'm sorry, Jody! I didn't mean it!"

Jody recognized Hunk's voice.

The stars stopped blinking, and Jody opened his eyes. Hunk was kneeling in front of him, his brown eyes wide with worry. Beside him was Coach Fisher.

"Feel better, Jody?"

"Yes. I feel okay." The coach helped him to his feet.

"I'll have a runner for you," said the coach.

But Jody put the helmet back on and trotted to first. "I'll be all right, Coach," he said. "I can run."

"Are you sure?" Coach Fisher looked at him anxiously.

Jody grinned. "I'm sure," he said.

Then he saw that the manager of the Gophers was removing Hunk Peters from the game and was putting in a left-hander. The southpaw warmed up for a while; then the game resumed.

The Dolphins' fans yelled loud and hard for Roddie Nelson to get a hit. They needed a run to tie the score, two runs to put them ahead.

A ball was called, and then a strike. Now Roddie got ready for the pitch he wanted. The ball breezed in, chest-high. Roddie swung. *Crack!* The ball arced out to short right field. The Gophers' second base-man and right fielder both raced after it. Jody stopped about a third of the way to second, waiting to see if the ball would be caught.

"I got it!" yelled the second baseman, running hard.

He had his gloved hand stretched out to receive the ball. He caught it and whirled to throw to first. Jody sped back in time.

The crowd cheered the Gophers' second baseman. Even the Dolphins' fans applauded him. It was a great catch.

Moonie came to the plate. Once again the fans greeted him with applause. He took a called strike, then belted a sizzling grounder to second. The second baseman bobbled the ball, and both Jody and Moonie were safe.

Lead-off man Duane West came up next. The two runs the Dolphins needed to get back into the lead were on first and second.

The Gophers' left-hander stepped to the mound, checked the runners, then threw. He had speed and pretty good control. He threw four pitches — one ball, and the rest strikes. Duane went down swinging.

Two outs.

Mike Brink took a called strike, then fouled two pitches in a row. The south-paw threw his next pitches low and inside. Mike waited; then the count was three and two.

"This is it, Mike!" Coach Fisher yelled. "Make it be in there!"

The ball breezed in, knee-high. Mike swung. *Crack!* A hot grounder to short. The shortstop caught the hop, tossed the ball to third, and Jody was out.

The game was over. The Gophers were the winners: 8–7.

❊   ❊   ❊

Rabbit was back in the game Thursday. The Dolphins were playing the Tigers again, the last game of the first series.

Rabbit had healed well. The welt had disappeared from his head. And he was doing fine at short, too. By the third inning he had handled five grounders without an error and had assisted with five put-outs.

As for Jody, he wasn't doing *anything* right. Two men had already stolen second on him. One had even stolen third. On that play Jody had almost thrown the man out, but *almost* wasn't good enough.

However, it was at the plate that something strange had really happened to Jody.

The first time up, he had swung at the first pitch and popped out. Nobody knew how he really felt then. He was glad he didn't have to spend a longer time at the plate.

Now he was up again. Johnny Bartho was

on third, and Joe Bell on second. The Tigers were leading, 3–2.

Jim Gregg, the Tigers' tall, wiry right-hander, hurled in the first pitch. It came in belt-high. Jody watched it, and all at once he thought it was streaking at him. He got scared and jumped back from the plate.

"Strike!" yelled the umpire.

The next pitch was slightly higher and just as close. Again Jody jumped back.

"Strike two!" yelled the umpire.

The Tigers' players started to laugh and make fun of him. His teammates shouted at him to swing. "Come on, Jody! You can hit him!" yelled Coach Fisher from his third-base coaching box.

Jody stepped out of the batter's box a moment, rubbed dust on his hands, then stepped back in again. Sweat stood out on his forehead and rolled in tiny rivers down his face.

"Stick in there, Jody, boy!" a voice said from the grandstand. "Don't be afraid of them!"

Jody remembered that voice. It belonged to the man who had been so friendly toward him during those first few games.

In came the pitch. It was knee-high. It was going to groove the middle of the plate. Jody could see that — *yet his right foot stepped back away from the plate as he swung. He missed the ball by a foot!*

That made the third out. Jody saw Johnny Bartho kick the third-base sack as he turned and headed for left field.

Jody tossed his bat aside and began putting on his shin guards. His hands shook. He had trouble fastening the buckles. Coach Fisher came over and helped him.

"What happened, Jody?" he asked quietly. "You looked scared up there."

"I know," said Jody.

43

"No sense being scared. Just stay in there. Forget what happened the other day. Make up your mind you're going to hit that ball. You've hit it before — you'll hit it again."

In the sixth Jody was up again. The score was 4–2 in the Tigers' favor. Birdie Davis was on first.

Jody waited out the pitcher. He got three balls on him, then a strike. *I wish he walks me, I wish he walks me,* Jody was telling himself.

"Strike two!" yelled the umpire.

Three and two. This would be it. He had to watch this next pitch closely.

The ball came in. It looked good, almost even with the letters on his jersey. Then all at once it seemed to come at his head. He ducked back, almost losing his balance.

"Yeaaa!" yelled the umpire. "You're out!"

Jody clamped his lips lightly for a moment, then walked away.

When the game was over, the score was the same, 4–2. As the teams walked off the field, Jody kept his eyes lowered so that he wouldn't have to look at anyone.

Suddenly he heard someone say, "Jody! Wait! I'd like to see you a minute!"

7

Jody turned and saw the tall, thin man who had become one of his best fans.

"Hi, Jody," the man greeted. "See that you have more troubles now, haven't you?"

"Guess so," said Jody, and began rubbing the toe of his right shoe into the grass.

"Two problems," said the man. "That's pretty rough going. Not throwing well and being afraid of a pitched ball are two of the worst things a ballplayer could wish for himself."

"I know," said Jody. "Guess I'll never be any different."

The man chuckled. "That's where you're wrong. You see, you do have a strong arm. You're just afraid to throw hard — you think you'll throw the ball *too* far. That's wrong thinking.

"Your new problem is worse. You can't be afraid of a pitched ball, because then you'll *never* hit. But you have hit, before — and very well, too. That bang you got on the head the other day scared you. You must forget that. That's why ballplayers wear helmets nowadays. When I played ball, we didn't even think of helmets. So — don't be afraid anymore. How about it?"

Jody smiled. "Okay."

The man walked away.

"Who is that?" Jody asked Roddie, who had stopped to wait for him. "He comes to most of our games."

"Jim somebody," said Roddie. "He's a

47

friend of Coach Fisher's. What was he saying to you?"

Jody told him as they went on their way home.

As days went by so did ball games. Jody showed improvement in his ball throwing, but not in his hitting. In two games he had poked out only one hit, and that was a blooper over second. Coach Fisher moved him from seventh to last place in the batting order. In the last two games the coach took him out in the fourth inning and had Rabbit Foote catch.

One day during practice Jim drove up alongside the ballpark and came onto the field. He sat in the stands and watched the Dolphins practice.

Jody caught his eye and smiled. Jim smiled back and waved.

At bat, Jody remembered what Jim had advised him about not being afraid of a pitched ball, because the helmet would protect him; that's why he wore it.

He recalled the bang on the head from a pitched ball. He forgot if it had hurt or not. Guess it wasn't the pain he was afraid of, anyway. He was just afraid of being hit, that's all. He *tried* not to be. But when he stood at the plate he just couldn't help it. He couldn't help it now. He stepped "into the bucket" each time the ball came in instead of stepping straight forward. He was hitting the ball, but not at all as he used to before he had been hit on the head.

"Hey, Jack!" Jim yelled suddenly from the stands. "How about letting me throw in a few?"

"Sure, Jim," said the coach. "Come on."

"Stay there, Jody!" cried Jim. "Let me throw to you."

Jim came in and put on the glove Coach Fisher handed him. He warmed up first, then began throwing to Jody.

With each pitch Jody's right foot moved back. He was pulling himself back, too.

"Stay in there, Jody," said Jim. "I won't hit you."

Almost all the pitches were over the plate. Jim certainly had marvelous control. Jody tried hard to step straight ahead when he swung. Each time he felt a strong urge inside him to pull away from the pitch. It was as if something were *making* him do that.

He hit a couple of grounders, missed a few pitches, and lined one over first. Then he bunted one down the third-base line.

Jim grinned at him. "You're coming around fine, Jody!" he said.

After practice was over, Jim talked to Coach Fisher a few moments. Jody saw the coach nod.

"Jody, Frank, Duane, and Birdie" — Coach Fisher snapped off the names — "stick around! Jim wants to work with you awhile!"

The other boys left — all except Johnny Bartho and Moonie Myers, who sat on the bench to watch.

Jody wondered what Jim intended to do. In a moment he found out. Jim ordered each player to his regular position, then had them throw the ball to each other. That was all they did. They just threw. He had Jody do the most throwing, making him throw hard to first, second, and third.

Jody's first throws were weak. Gradually he improved. Sometimes his throws were over the baseman's head. But he was doing much better than he had done in any game.

"This gets me," Jody heard Moonie grumble from the bench. "What's he spending all his time on Sinclair for? He's just wasting his time for nothing!"

"That's just what I was thinking," said Johnny. "Come on. Let's go home."

Early Friday morning Jody and Midnight left the house and walked down the street. They were going to the lake about two miles away, to sit on Flatiron Rock and watch the ducks for a while, and then come back.

Suddenly a voice yelled out: "Jody! Wait a minute!"

Jody turned. Coming around the corner of the street he had just passed was Johnny Bartho. Johnny had started toward him at a run.

Jody waited, a little bit puzzled. Johnny was seldom without Moonie.

Johnny pulled up alongside him, scuffing his shoes so that he made Midnight jump with fright. He was carrying a flashlight.

"Hi," he said. "Where are you going?"

"To Flatiron Rock," replied Jody. "Midnight and I go there once in a while."

"You *and Midnight?*" Johnny looked down at the cat. "I've heard of guys being good friends with dogs, but never with cats."

"You get them trained, they're as smart as dogs," said Jody.

He started walking again, and Midnight began trotting beside him. If Johnny wanted to come along, okay. But he wasn't going to ask him. He could still remember Johnny and Moonie talking about him at the games and practices, and none of it was any good.

"I asked Moonie if he'd want to go to Indian Cave today, but he can't," Johnny said. "You ever been there?"

"Of course," said Jody. "Many times." He

shrugged. "Well — three or four times, I guess."

"Ever been *inside*?"

"Well, no," said Jody. "Never inside. Never *far* inside, I mean." He looked curiously at Johnny. "Why? Is that where you're going? Is that why you have that flashlight?"

Johnny smiled, "Yes. You want to go? It's not far from here, and we can go inside and explore. I found two arrowheads in there once. Moonie found one, too. Of course, we had to go in a long ways. You're not scared, are you?"

"No," Jody said. "I'll go with you. What's there to be scared of?"

They walked a quarter of a mile down the road to a wooden bridge. They stepped off the road and slid down the steep bank to the edge of a creek.

The boys walked up alongside the creek, Midnight following close behind. They reached falls that were about ten feet high and two feet wide. They climbed the rocky ledge that was like steps beside it. They reached the top. Here the creek was wide but the water was very shallow.

The cave was a big hole in the hillside to the left.

"Here we are!" said Johnny. "Watch that crack in the floor. There's water in it."

They rested for a while on a large rock. Then Johnny turned on his flashlight and started to walk deeper into the cave. A chill crawled along Jody's spine as he followed at Johnny's heels.

"Meow!" said Midnight. He hesitated awhile, then trotted in after them.

"Look at that," said Johnny.

He was shining the flashlight against the wall. Into the flat surface of a huge rock were carved pictures of a tepee and of a

Native American chief. Jody wondered how long those had been there. Maybe scientists knew, he thought. Or those people who studied Native American lore.

They walked farther in. I wonder how far he's going, Jody thought.

"Scared?" asked Johnny.

"No," said Jody. "Why should I be scared?"

He was scared, but he wasn't going to let Johnny know it. Not for one second.

Suddenly his left foot slipped on a slimy rock. He fell to his knee and let out a cry. Johnny turned, flashed the light on him, then on the rock beside him.

Jody's heart flipped. Not a foot away from him was a pool of water. The water was about four feet below the floor of the cave. It looked deep and dangerous. Jody shuddered as he rose slowly to his feet.

"I'm sorry," said Johnny. "I knew the pool

was here somewhere, but I didn't see it either. We'll go to the falls, then turn back."

Jody soon heard the hum coming from farther inside the cave. They walked on for another fifty feet, the hum of the falls growing louder all the time. And then Johnny shone the flashlight straight ahead, and Jody saw the falls. The water looked like a huge white curtain. He couldn't see the bottom of it. From where they stood all they could see was the spray that leaped up, and all they could hear was its thundering noise.

The whole thing was creepy. Jody felt goose bumps on his arms.

They started back, walking side by side now. Johnny talked almost all the way back, telling about the Native Americans and how they had fought the pioneers, and about Daniel Boone and Davy Crockett.

At last Jody saw the round hole of daylight

ahead. A little while later they were out of the cave.

"Aren't you glad you came with me?" Johnny said with a smile.

"Sure am," replied Jody, smiling back. "Sometime I'm going again."

Just then he saw Midnight scooting back into the cave.

"Midnight!" yelled Jody. "Come back here!"

"He's chasing a rat or something," said Johnny. "I saw it run ahead in front of him. Don't worry. He'll be back."

They waited. After a few minutes Midnight didn't come back, and Jody became worried. Was it really a rat Midnight had chased, or was it something else?

"I'm going in after him," he said.

"Well, I'm not," said Johnny. "I don't have any love for cats. Here. Take my flashlight. I'll wait for you out here."

Jody took the flashlight and went into the cave. "Midnight!" he called. "Midnight! Come here, pal!"

Midnight didn't come.

Jody walked farther into the cave. Every few seconds he would call out Midnight's name. At last he heard an answer: *Meow! Meow!*

"Midnight!" Jody cried. "Midnight! Come here!"

Still Midnight did not come. But Jody kept hearing him.

And then Jody started running forward. He knew what had happened.

He reached the pool, shone the flashlight into it. There was Midnight, unable to get out. And there was another animal. It looked like a rat, but Jody wasn't sure.

"Midnight!" Jody scolded. "See what happens when you run away from me?"

He got on his knees and reached down. He stretched his arms as far as he could, but he couldn't reach far enough.

"Midnight!" sobbed Jody. Tears burned in his throat. "I can't reach you!"

9

Jody pushed himself to his knees. A lump filled his throat. He swallowed, but the lump remained.

Midnight sure had gotten into a mess this time! But it wasn't all his fault. He liked to chase mice and other animals that were smaller than he was. This time he had gone too far.

How was Jody going to get his cat out of that pool? There was a wall all around it. The water flowed in through a deep narrow crack in the rock floor, and it flowed out through a deep narrow crack. It was impossible for Midnight to crawl out by himself. He tried, but he kept sliding back into the water.

What was worse, Jody could not get him out either.

I can't leave him there! Jody thought. *I can't let him drown! But how am I going to get him out? If I ran back for a net, he'd be drowned by the time I got back!*

A net? Suddenly the thought gave him another idea. His sweater!

His hands trembled as he laid the flashlight on the dry rock floor beside him and hurriedly slipped off his sweater. Then, while he held the flashlight in one hand, he leaned over the edge of the pool again and held the sweater down with his other hand.

"Come here, Midnight," he pleaded softly. "Come here, pal. Grab hold of my sweater."

Midnight was still swimming around, his

black fur matted against him like a shiny coat.

Jody kept calling to him to grab hold of the sweater. Midnight did not seem to hear him. Or maybe he didn't understand.

"Midnight, listen to me. Put your claws into my sweater. It's the only way, Midnight. The only way. Please!"

Midnight was clawing at the wall at Jody's left. He fell back and tried again, a little closer to Jody this time. Again he fell back, his head going under the water so that for a moment he was completely out of sight. Once more his head popped up, and he began swimming hard to keep afloat.

"Midnight! Here, pal!" Jody flashed the light onto the sweater.

Midnight looked at the sweater. He swam toward it, sank one claw into it. Then he sank another claw into it. Jody felt the sweater stretch. He grabbed a stronger hold of it and slowly began to pull it up, with Midnight clinging on.

"Just a little more, Midnight!" he whispered. "Hang on a little more!"

A moment later he put his left arm around his cat and lifted him into his arms.

"Midnight! My pal!" he cried. He hugged the cat tenderly to him while his heart spilled over with joy. "Come on! Let's get out of here!"

He carried Midnight out with him.

When he reached the outside Jody returned the flashlight to Johnny and began drying off Midnight with his sweater. Johnny's eyes were like marbles as he looked at the cat.

"What happened to him?" he asked.

"Chased a rat right into the pool," said Jody.

Johnny looked at the front of Jody's shirt and pants. "You're soaked," he said. "Did you have to pull him out?"

"I tried, but I couldn't reach him," Jody said. "Then I pulled him out with my sweater."

Johnny stared at him. He didn't say anything for a long time, even when Jody started down the hillside, Midnight trailing at his heels.

On their way into town they met Moonie, Duane, and Frank. The boys wanted to know where Jody and Johnny had been, and Johnny told them. Then he told them about Jody's cat chasing a rat or something into the cave and right into the pool, and how Jody saved the cat by pulling it out with his sweater.

The boys laughed. They thought it was funny. Jody didn't want to hear any more about it, and started to walk away.

"Why did you have to laugh?" Johnny Bartho snapped angrily. "Would you have thought of using your sweater to save a cat? I probably would have let it drown. You probably would have, too!"

Jody turned and stared at Johnny. He couldn't believe that it was Johnny Bartho talking like that about him and Midnight. Johnny Bartho, Moonie Myers's best friend!

"Cats!" jeered Moonie. "I wouldn't give a nickel for one!"

Jody flushed. He looked directly into Moonie's eyes.

"I'm glad you said that, Moonie. You don't deserve a cat. You don't deserve any kind of pet!"

Jody spun and walked hurriedly away. He felt good that he had told Moonie off.

There was batting practice at 5:30. Coach Fisher was throwing. His pitches were not always down the groove — some of them were wide, some were inside. Jody was batting. He took a cautious step back with his right foot from each pitch.

"Stay in there, Jody," said the coach. "You're putting that right foot in the bucket."

"Sure he is!" said Moonie loudly from near first base where he was playing catch with Johnny Bartho. "He's scared! Why don't you get up closer and toss the ball underhand to him, Coach? Maybe he'd hit it then!"

Jody's face turned a deep red.

This was the first time Moonie had spoken to him since this morning. He knew Moonie was sore. Moonie had not liked it when Jody had told him that he did not deserve a pet.

Jody also figured that Moonie was jealous because Johnny Bartho had taken him and

Midnight into Indian Cave. Now Moonie was trying to get even. He wanted to shame Jody in front of Coach Fisher and everyone else.

But Coach Fisher was looking hard at Moonie. "One more wisecrack like that, Moonie," he said, "and you'll turn in your uniform. Never let me hear you talk like that again." He turned back to Jody. "Okay, Jody. Stick in there. Step into the pitch, not away from it. You'll gain your confidence again. Don't worry."

He stepped on the mound and threw. Jody held his jaws firmly together as he watched the ball come in. He tried to forget about Moonie and think only of Coach Fisher's words: *Step into the pitch, not away from it.*

He did just that. The ball came close, but as it started by him he saw that there was still plenty of space between it and him. He was sure it could cut the inside corner of the plate for a strike if he didn't swing.

He swung. *Crack!* The bat met the ball solidly and sailed over first baseman Birdie Davis's head for a clean hit.

"Thataboy, Jody!" said the coach. "Just step into it. That's all you have to do."

Old-Timers' Day! The day when men who used to play baseball, but were too old to play any more, got two teams together and played each other. The money that was donated would be for bats, balls, and other needed equipment for the Little Leaguers.

It was July 28, Saturday afternoon. The weather was ideal for baseball. The field was in excellent shape. Several men, including Jody's father and Coach Fisher, had been working on it this morning.

"Make sure every stone is cleared away,

no matter how little it is," Coach Fisher had said, laughing. "We can't take a chance on bad hops!"

The bleachers were filled with fans. Many brought their own lawn chairs on which they could sit to watch the game comfortably. A stand was set up near left field for ice-cold pop and hot dogs.

All the league teams were assembled at the game. They sat wherever they wanted to. Most of the Dolphins' team were sitting on the top seat of the bleachers behind first base. Jody was sitting next to Rabbit Foote, grinning happily. He hadn't seen Dad play baseball since that first Old-Timers' Day game three years ago. And that was so long ago he could hardly remember it.

He tried to pick out as many of the players as he could. He recognized Rabbit's father and Terry McClane's. But that was all. He didn't know any of the other boys' fathers. He saw Jim, too. Wonder what position he played?

Names were given to the teams. One was the Reds, the other the Blues. Jody's father played on the Reds' team.

The game started, and the crowd began yelling. Mr. Sinclair was on first. His uniform fit him like a glove. Especially his pants. But that wasn't unusual. The uniforms were tight on most of the bigger men.

The first man up punched a looping single over second, and the crowd cheered. The second batter tried to lay down a bunt, but fouled. Then he hit a high bouncing grounder to short. The shortstop caught the hop, threw it to second for the force-out, and the second baseman snapped it to first. A double play!

Mr. Sinclair really had stretched far out

for the throw, and Jody smiled. Dad really didn't look bad there at all!

The third hitter clouted the pitch far out to center. The center fielder misjudged the ball, and the hitter got two bases. He could have gone to third, but he was a big man, gray-haired, and he looked too tired to run any farther.

The crowd laughed and applauded him.

The next hitter was left-handed. He belted a grounder down to first. Mr. Sinclair caught it, made the put-out himself, and half an inning was over.

Jody saw Jim run out to center field. The way he runs I bet he could cover a lot of ground even now, thought Jody.

The Reds came to bat. A single and an error gave them a chance to score. Rabbit Foote's father was third hitter, and he clouted the pitch for a double. He was short and fast — just like his son Rabbit — and if the second runner had not stopped on third Mr. Foote would have gone on to third himself.

Two more runs came in, and Mr. Sinclair came to the plate. He let a strike go by, then belted a long fly to left. It was mighty high. But the left fielder moved under it and caught it.

"Nice hit, anyway, Dad!" yelled Jody.

Jody was anxious to see Jim hit. He seemed to know a great deal about baseball. By the size of him, he might even drive one over that left-field fence. But Jim didn't get up to bat until the next inning.

There were men on second and third when he came to the plate.

"Come on, Jim! the fans yelled. "Knock those men in!"

The pitcher stepped on the mound, checked the runners, and delivered. The ball came in, chest-high. Jim, a right-hander, made a motion to swing. Then he moved back from the plate.

"Strike!" said the umpire.

"Come on, Jim!" one of his teammates yelled. "Stay in there! It won't hit you!"

The second pitch came in. Jim stepped back with his left foot again.

The crowd laughed. Rabbit Foote and some of the players laughed, too. Jody didn't. He just sat there staring at Jim.

The umpire called the next two pitches balls. The next was a strike. Jim swung at it and missed it by a foot. You could tell he was afraid of the pitch.

I don't believe it! thought Jody. *And he's the one who keeps telling me not to be afraid!*

"Rabbit," said Jody, "everyone calls him Jim. What's his last name?"

Rabbit looked at him. "You don't know?"

"No, I don't," said Jody.

Rabbit jerked his thumb at the boy beside him. Jody leaned forward and looked at Moonie Myers — Moonie, whose face was red as a beet, and who was the only boy on the top seat besides Jody who wasn't laughing.

"That's Mr. Myers," said Rabbit. "Moonie's father."

Jody was stunned. Moonie's father . . . no wonder he came to all the games! No wonder he always had a carload of kids with him. Jody had never really thought much about who he was. He had just figured that he was a good Dolphins' fan.

"Strike three!"

Mr. Myers went down swinging. It was an awkward swing, as if he had decided to cut at the ball at the very last moment.

The crowd roared. A lot of the fans poked fun at him. It was happy fun. Nobody was serious. But still, the way Mr. Myers turned away from the plate and walked to the dugout, anybody could tell he was far from happy.

Jody took another look at Moonie. Moonie was sitting like a statue. He was staring straight ahead, his arms crossed. A couple of other kids looked at him, too. But Moonie didn't move a muscle.

Two innings went by, and Mr. Myers was up again. There was a man on first base, and no outs.

"Let's get two!" Jody's father yelled as he stood in front of the first-base bag, holding the runner on.

The first pitch breezed in, and Mr. Myers moved back from it.

"Strike!"

The fans laughed and poked fun at Mr. Myers again. Jody looked at the faces around him. Some of them looked sorry for Mr. Myers. But most of them just thought it was very funny that Mr. Myers was afraid of the pitches.

"*Stay in there, Jim! Hit it!*"

The folks sitting in front of Jody looked around at him and smiled. Rabbit grinned at him, too, and poked him lightly in the ribs. His face turned red a little. He really hadn't meant to yell out like that.

He saw Mr. Myers dig his toes into the dirt, tap the bat against the plate, and then hold it above his shoulder. The pitch came in, and Mr. Myers didn't move his feet an inch.

Two more pitches whipped in and Mr. Myers just stood there watching them.

"What're you waiting for, Jim?" somebody yelled. "Get that bat off your shoulder!"

"Hit it, Mr. Myers!" Jody whispered to himself. "Hit it! Show 'em you're not afraid!"

The pitch came in. Mr. Myers moved his

foot forward and swung. *Crack!* The ball sailed out like a ship over the second baseman's head for a clean hit. The runner on first went around to third. Mr. Myers made his turn at first, then went back to the bag, a happy, proud smile on his face.

The fans cheered. It was the loudest noise they had made since the game had started. Jody, Rabbit, and all the kids on the top row stood up and clapped thunderously. All . . . except Moonie.

"Come on, Moonie!" cried Rabbit. "Give your dad a hand! That was a beautiful hit!"

Moonie's face colored. His eyes blinked a couple of times, and then a smile burst over his face. He stood up and began to clap as hard as he could.

"Thataboy, Dad!" he shouted. "Thataboy!"

The game ended with the Blues winning, 7–6.

✿   ✿   ✿

The boys walked out of the ballpark and began to talk about Mr. Myers's being afraid of a pitched ball and about that nice single he had hit.

"He's just like you, Jody," Frank York said. "Maybe that's why he always tries to help you when you bat. You've been awful scared of those pitches, too, ever since you got beaned."

Jody nodded. "Could be," he said.

"Did your dad get beaned sometime when he was playing baseball, Moonie?" Frank asked.

Moonie shrugged. "I don't know. If he did, he never told me."

They kept talking about their fathers. Jody learned some things he had never known before: that some of them had played with teams in the International League, which was just one jump below the major leagues. His own dad had played semipro.

✿   ✿   ✿

They were approaching Jody's house when he heard a dog barking loudly nearby. The boys stopped talking and looked for the dog.

"There he is," Johnny Bartho pointed. "At the bottom of that pole."

They saw a German shepherd standing at the foot of the light pole in front of Jody's house. He was looking up at something on the pole and barking his head off.

Jody looked up to see what he was barking at. A cry started in his throat, then stuck there.

Sitting on the very top of the pole was Midnight!

12

The German shepherd belonged to the Slater family, who lived two blocks away. He was kept in their yard most of the time, but sometimes he would leave and roam the neighborhood. His name was Firpo.

"Firpo!" Jody shouted. "Get away from here! Go on home!"

The big dog merely looked at him, then kept barking at Midnight.

Johnny Bartho picked up a large stone and threw it at the dog. It missed Firpo by inches.

"Don't!" said Jody. "You might hurt him. I'll get him away from here."

Cautiously, he started walking toward the big dog.

"Careful, Jody," warned Rabbit. "He might bite."

"He's not dangerous," said Jody. "I've been close to him before."

Slowly he walked up to the dog, talking softly all the while. "Come here, Firpo. Come here, boy."

Firpo stopped barking and looked at him. As Jody approached him, Firpo stepped away. He barked a few more times, but now his bark was only half as loud as it was before.

"Come here, Firpo," said Jody quietly. "Let me take you home."

Firpo stopped moving and began to wag his long tail. His ears stood up straight and his tongue hung out of his opened mouth. He was looking directly at Jody, and he didn't seem dangerous at all. Jody took hold of his collar and gently led him down the street.

Behind him he heard the boys laughing. "Well, how do you like that?" said Johnny. "Who said Jody Sinclair hasn't got nerve?"

Jody took Firpo home, then ran all the way back. Midnight was still on top of the pole. He was like a fluffy black ball. Only his head and his shining eyes moved.

"We tried to call him," said Moonie, "but he won't budge."

Jody looked up. There were six wires on the crossbars of the pole, just a couple of feet under Midnight. Dangerous wires that could mean death. Jody was reminded of the trip back from Lincoln Park when they were trapped by the same kind of electric wires. The thought made him shudder.

"Jody," Johnny Bartho said suddenly, "Moonie's dad works for the telephone company. He has climbers. He can bring Midnight down. Can't he, Moonie?"

Moonie shrugged. "He doesn't climb poles any more."

"But he can still get a pair, can't he?" Johnny said.

Jody wiped sweat from his brow. "Maybe he wouldn't want to climb that high up," he said. "And those wires. They could be real dangerous. Maybe he wouldn't want to take a chance."

"Oh, sure, he will," said Johnny. "I'll go ask him. Okay, Moonie?"

Moonie stood there a moment, chewing on his lower lip and thinking. "I'll go," he said then.

Just then Jody's dad and mom stepped out of the house. Mr. Sinclair's hair was uncombed, and he was wearing only his pants and a T-shirt. Jody knew he must have just finished taking a shower.

"What's going on, boys?" he asked.

"Midnight's on top of the pole, Dad," Jody said. "Firpo chased him up there. Moonie was just going to call his dad to bring some climbers."

Mr. Sinclair came off the porch and looked up the pole at Midnight. "Can you beat that?" he said.

"*Meow!*" said Midnight.

"That's a job for the SPCA," suggested Mr. Sinclair. "They have experts who handle jobs like this. No need to bother Jim. Anyway," he chuckled, "after that hit he got he wouldn't feel like climbing a light pole!"

"That's right! The SPCA!" said Jody. "I'd forgot all about them!"

Mr. Sinclair put in a call to the Society for the Prevention of Cruelty to Animals.

Within an hour a man drove into the driveway in a pickup truck. The boys pointed at Midnight, sitting on top of the pole. They watched the man put on his climbers and a long pair of gloves and climb up the pole. Nobody made a sound as the man put his gloved hand around Midnight, clutched him by the back of his neck, and lifted him off the pole.

Midnight let out a loud *"Meowr!"* and started to claw at the air with his paws. But the man had him well under control. He climbed down the pole with Midnight. When he reached the ground, he handed Midnight to Jody, and Jody hugged him fiercely.

Jody thanked the man, who smiled and left. Mom and Dad went back into the house. Johnny Bartho and the other boys departed, too. Only Jody and Moonie remained.

"Moonie," Jody said. "I want to thank you, anyway, for wanting to go after your father."

Moonie shrugged. "That's okay, Jody. I think he would have been glad to rescue Midnight for you. He likes you a lot."

"I know," said Jody. "I like him, too."

"Jody, how about playing catch?"

"Okay. I'll go in and get a ball and a couple of gloves."

He brought out his own glove and the one Dad had. They started playing catch.

The very first ball Jody pitched was a looping throw that barely reached Moonie.

"Oh, come on, Jody. Throw 'em up, will you?"

Jody tried again, and again Moonie had to rush forward a few steps to catch the ball before it hit the ground.

"I don't know, Jody," said Moonie, shaking his head. "I don't think you'll ever be able to throw."

Jody had forgotten all about his poor throwing. Now that he was reminded of it, he became worried all over again.

He had twice the problem Mr. Myers had! Mr. Myers was only afraid of a pitched ball. He, Jody, was afraid of a pitched ball — *and* he couldn't throw.

13

Throw that ball! Hit me on the head with it! What are you afraid of? Hurting my hand?"

It was Jim Myers talking. He was on the mound, Jody was behind the plate, and Moonie was on second. Jody didn't have his catching equipment on. All they were doing was throwing the ball. Jim would hurl it to Jody, and Jody would either throw it back to him or to Moonie.

He was doing better than he had all season. The ball snapped from his hand like a shot. He was throwing accurately, too, right at Jim Myers's head. And, when he pegged it to Moonie, the ball whipped through the air directly into Moonie's glove almost every time.

After a half an hour of this throwing practice, Jim and the boys pulled the batting cage up behind the plate. Then Jim Myers had Jody put on a helmet and pick up a bat.

"Stay in that box and don't move," said Jim Myers. "Watch some of those balls go by. Look them over as well as you can." He grinned. "Remember what you yelled to me at the Old-Timers' game? 'Stay in there!' you said. Well, I stood in there. Now let me see *you* do it. . . . Okay, son. Pitch 'em in."

Moonie pitched them in. Jody stood in the batting box, his bat held high over his shoulder. He watched the first ball come in and goose pimples popped out on his arms. But he stood there, and the ball zipped by and hit the batting cage. Moonie pitched in a dozen balls. Twice Jody was tempted to dodge back. But the ball breezed by him, missing him by almost a foot.

"Fine!" said Jim Myers. "Okay, now. Let's see you hit it, Jody. Just take a short step forward."

A half a dozen neighborhood kids were in the outfield. They all had gloves. Jody began swinging, taking a short step forward as Jim Myers had advised him to do. Gradually he began to hit the ball. Gradually he began to feel more comfortable at the plate. He kept hitting until he was tired, then he pitched to Moonie for a while.

"Okay," said Jim Myers. "We'll do this every day between practices and games. Can you be here tomorrow evening, Jody?"

Jody thought a little. "We play the Bears tomorrow," he said.

"Okay. Make it the next day, then," Jim Myers said with a grin.

Jody smiled. "Okay!" he said.

He felt good. Mr. Myers was sure a great guy! Imagine him taking such an interest in a boy that he was willing to sacrifice a lot of his time just to make this boy be a better thrower and hitter.

On August 2, just before the Moose game, Coach Jack Fisher called his team together.

"We have one more game to play after today's," he said. "If we win today, we'll have a good chance to be in the play-off. We've been doing quite well all season, considering that most of you boys have played little before."

He cleared his throat and looked at Jody. "Jody, we'll start Rabbit at catching today. You've been starting to hit again, but the Moose have some good hitters who are fast on bases. They'll take advantage of you every time they get on. You are throwing better than you did at the start of the season. Don't get me wrong. But against these boys you must do even better. I think, with Rabbit catching, they won't dare to run as much."

"Who's playing short?" Moonie asked.

"Joe Bell," said the coach.

"Isn't Jody going to play at all?"

"Not today."

Jody looked across at Moonie. Their eyes locked. Then Jody looked down at the ground. He thought about all the hours he had spent practicing batting and throwing. He had improved a lot. He was sure of it. It wasn't fair that Coach Fisher wasn't letting him play today.

"Infielders, hustle out there. Rabbit, warm up Moonie. We have only a few minutes left."

Moonie took his time on the mound. He pitched hard and had the Moose swinging and missing. He mowed down the first two with strikeouts. He was a little wild on the third hitter, and walked him. Then the Moose cleanup man, Mel Devlin, stepped to the plate, and the Moose fans began giving him support from the bleachers.

Mel was tall and thin. He held up his bat as if it were a toothpick. He had five home runs this year so far. One of them had been against Moonie during the early part of the season.

From the bench, Jody watched eagerly. He remembered those pitches Mel had hit. They had been high ones, right across the letters of his shirt.

Keep them low, Moonie, Jody thought. *Right around his knees.*

Moonie toed the rubber and pitched. The pitch was high — *straight across the letters on Mel's shirt.* Mel swung with all his might. *Crack!* The bat met the ball solidly. The white pill streaked like a missile to left field.

But it was curving! It was going . . .

"Foul!" cried the umpire.

The Moose fans groaned.

The Dolphins' fans cried, "Just one long strike, Moonie, ol' boy!"

Jody's heart thudded. Man, that was close. *Come on, Moonie! Keep them low!*

Moonie kept working hard on Mel. He gave no more high ones. But neither did he throw him another strike. Mel got a free ticket to first base.

Moonie had trouble with the next batter. The hitter fouled three pitches in a row. Then Moonie curved him, and the batter swished out.

"Nice going Moonie," said the coach. "Three strikeouts that first inning. Keep it up. You're doing fine."

The Dolphins didn't get a hit during their turn at bat. The Moose came back and threatened again. They got a man on. A sacrifice bunt put him on second. A long fly to right field was caught, but the runner tagged up and made it safely to third.

Two outs. The Dolphins' infield played deep. Moonie stretched, delivered, and a grounder was hit to short. Joe Bell charged in after it. He fumbled it! The ball skittered behind him. He picked it up, fired it to first.

Safe! And the runner scored.

The next hitter popped to first, and the side was retired.

The innings moved quickly. The Moose put two more runs across in the top of the third. In the bottom of the fourth Roddie tripled, and Duane drove him in with a hard single over second base.

Moonie then stepped to the plate and pounded a smashing drive to right center field. Duane raced to second, to third, and then tried to score.

"Hit it!" Frank York, who was next batter, yelled at him.

Duane slid. The throw from deep second base was almost perfect. The catcher caught the ball, put it on Duane, and the umpire yelled, "Out!"

Moonie took his turn at second and then returned and stayed there.

"Let's keep it going!" yelled Coach Fisher. "Swing at 'em, Frankie!"

Frankie waited for the pitch he wanted. He swung. A single! Moonie came all the way in to score, making it two runs for the Dolphins.

Then Arnie struck out to end the rally.

Score: Moose 3; Dolphins 2.

The Moose lead-off man pulled a surprise. He dragged the first pitch, bunting it down the third-base line. Duane ran in, tried to field the bunt, and slid. He got up disgustedly, tossed the ball to Moonie, and returned to his position. Only now he played in close, on the grass, in case the batter tried a sacrifice bunt.

The batter did! But he bunted the ball down the first-base line. It looked as if he, too, would get a hit out of it.

Birdie, also playing in close, charged in

after the bunt. He fielded it, turned, and whipped the ball to Moonie, who was running to cover first.

Out!

The Dolphins' fans cheered. "Nice play, Birdie!"

"That's the way to play heads-up ball, Moonie!"

One out, man on second.

Moonie stepped on the rubber. He took a quick look over his shoulder at the man leading off second, then delivered. *Crack!* A hard blow just over Frank York's head. Frank leaped. The ball barely grazed his glove. The runner on second made it to third and then bolted for home.

Roddie scooped up the ball in right field and heaved it. It was a good throw. It struck the ground twenty feet in front of home plate and bounced up into Rabbit's waiting mitt.

The runner hit the dirt and slid across the

plate just as Rabbit put the ball on him. It was close. Very close.

But the umpire's hands were spread out flat. And very clearly he shouted: "Safe!"

That was it for the Moose that inning. Now they led 4–2, and Jody didn't think the Dolphins had a chance. He was getting tired sitting on the bench, too. And worried. Would Coach Fisher ever let him catch again this year?

Birdie walked, and Johnny Bartho doubled, sending Birdie around to third.

Joe Bell, who was due for a hit, was up next. Coach Fisher gave him the squeeze signal. Joe tried twice to bunt, and both times fouled the pitches. On the next pitch he struck out.

Rabbit tossed aside one of the two bats he was holding and started for the plate.

"Rabbit, wait! Jody, hit in place of Rabbit!"

Jody looked up, surprised. Had he heard right? Had the coach spoken to him?

"Come on, Jody!" said the coach. "Let's hustle!"

"Yes, sir!" murmured Jody, and sprang out of the dugout.

15

Jody moved as if he were in a dream. He picked out his favorite bat and swung it back and forth a few times to limber his muscles. Then he stepped to the plate.

"Strike!" The first pitch was near his knees, and he backed up a little.

"Stay in there, Jody, boy!" someone yelled in the bleachers. "Be a hitter!"

His heart warmed. He knew whose voice that was. *I'm not afraid,* he thought. *I'm not.*

Another pitch. "Ball!"

Then it came in, letters-high. Curving in

toward him. He pulled back his bat and swung with everything he had.

Crack! The blow could be heard all round the field.

The ball sailed out to deep right field — over the fielder's head! It looked as if it would go over the fence. It didn't. It struck the grass in front of it, bounced up against the fence, and the fielder caught it. By the time he pegged it in, Birdie and Johnny had scored, and Jody was resting on third base.

"Beautiful hit, Jody!" yelled the coach. He ran forward and slapped him happily on the back. "You really blasted that one, fella!"

"Thanks," said Jody, breathing hard.

Roddie came up, socked a one-one pitch toward center field. It was a real high fly. Jody held up at third until the fielder caught the ball. Then he raced in as hard as he could, scoring easily.

Duane grounded out, and the rally was over. Three runs, and Jody had knocked in two of them himself and had scored the third. He felt just fine.

And that curve he had hit — he knew he'd never be afraid of a pitched ball any more.

The Moose came to bat for the last time. They were a beaten bunch. Moonie mowed down the first two hitters, and the third popped out to Jody.

The Dolphins won, 5–4.

They had won their chance to compete in the play-off game.

They beat the Gophers on Tuesday to clinch second place with ten wins and five losses. On Wednesday the Tigers walloped the

Bobcats to win first-place honors with twelve wins and only three losses.

The standings:

	WON	LOST	GAMES BEHIND
Tigers	12	3	—
Dolphins	10	5	2
Bobcats	8	7	4
Bears	6	9	6
Moose	5	10	7
Gophers	4	11	8

Now the two teams were to play each other for the championship. Coach Fisher was keeping Rabbit Foote behind the plate. Rabbit was doing all right. In the Gophers game he had thrown out two men who might have scored if they had stolen second safely. Coach had had Jody pinch-hit, though, and he had hit safely.

It was Jody's arm the coach was afraid of.

He couldn't trust Jody to throw that ball hard and straight when he really had to.

The Tigers started things rolling immediately. They began hitting Terry McClane, scoring two runs in the first and then two more in the second. The Dolphins got a run in the bottom of the second to make the score 4–1.

Then Terry bore down. He threw the ball across the corners, and the third inning went by without the Tigers' scoring.

Johnny blasted a long drive in the bottom of the third and scored on Joe Bell's single. The Tigers held them from scoring more that inning.

Then, in the top of the fourth, with Tigers on first and second, a terrible thing happened.

Rabbit's right thumb was split open by a foul tip.

Time was called, and Coach Fisher looked at the thumb. It was a nasty cut.

"Just patch it up, Coach," Rabbit said. "I can still play."

"I'll patch it up," replied the coach, "but you're not going to play." He looked around. His eyes spotted Jody. "Jody, help get those things off Rabbit and put them on yourself. Hurry it up."

Jody unbuckled the shin guards and buckled them on his own legs. Then Rabbit tossed him the chest protector and the mask.

"Good luck, Jody," he said.

"Thanks," said Jody.

Coach Fisher took Rabbit to the dugout, opened the first aid kit, and took care of Rabbit's thumb. On the field Jody was catching for Terry. He threw the ball twice into the dirt, then tried harder and threw the others perfectly. After eight pitches the umpire called time in, and the game resumed.

"Okay, boys!" the Tigers' fans began to yell. "Now's your chance! You can steal this catcher blind! That glass arm of his can't throw out a turtle!"

"Come on, boy! Come on, Terry! Slam it in here!" Jody rattled on like this. He hoped it would smother those awful things the opponents were yelling about him.

He caught Terry's first pitch, rising quickly to throw to third if he had to. But the runners remained on their bases.

"Come on! Steal!" someone in the bleachers yelled. "Let's see you steal on him!"

That voice! It wasn't the same one that had yelled the first time. That one wasn't familiar. This one was. It belonged to Mr. Myers. But why should Mr. Myers . . . ?

The pitch came in. From the corners of his eyes Jody could see the runners take off.

"Throw 'im out, Jody! Throw 'im out!"

Jody pegged the ball hard to third. The

ball shot like a white meteor. Duane caught it, pulled it down, and touched the runner sliding in.

"Out!" yelled the base umpire.

The Dolphins' fans screamed happily.

Jody could hear Mr. Myers laughing in the bleachers.

There was no more base-stealing that inning. And no more runs for the Tigers.

The Dolphins began blasting the ball and put across two runs to tie the score 4-all before the Tigers stopped them.

The Tigers came up in the fifth, the top of their batting order ready to gnaw the Dolphins to bits.

The first man walked, and once again the cry rose for the runner to steal.

"He can't throw to second! That glass arm broke when he threw to third!"

That was the Tigers' fan yelling.

"Sure! Try out that arm! See what happens!"

And that was Mr. Myers.

It was like a game those two men had up there in the bleachers, one sitting on the Tigers' side, the other on the Dolphins'.

The ball came in. The batter shifted his position in the batting box. He was going to bunt.

He met the ball squarely. It struck the ground in front of the plate, hopped twice, and Jody pounced on it. He picked it up, pegged it hard to second. Frank York caught it, stepped on the bag, and whipped the ball to first.

Twice the base umpire jerked up his thumb.

A double play!

"There you are!" yelled Mr. Myers. "There's your glass arm!"

The Dolphins' fans cheered, clapped, and stamped their feet on the bleachers' seats. The Tigers' fans only stared and shook their heads unbelievingly.

The next batter whiffed.

Jody was first batter for the Dolphins. Loud applause filled the stands as he stepped to the plate. He felt good. Real good.

He took a called strike, then knocked out a clothesline single over first. Roddie bunted him to second. Then Duane socked one into the opposite field for two bases. Jody scored. Terry singled, too. Duane was called out at home after a strong peg from the outfield. Frank popped out, and the inning was over.

The Tigers got men on, but they couldn't bring them in. The Dolphins won, 5–4.

Coach Fisher and all the rest of the Dolphins team crowded around Jody. They slapped him on the back and shook his hand and all talked at the same time.

When things quieted down a little, the coach said, "Nice game, Jody. You certainly came through when we needed you the most."

"Thanks, Coach," said Jody. "How's Rabbit's thumb?"

"Oh, it'll be all right." The coach grinned. "I patched it up fine."

Mr. Myers stepped forward and stretched out his hand.

"May I have the honor?" He smiled. "Guess you proved what that arm is *really* made of, didn't you, Jody?"

Jody took Mr. Myers's hand and smiled back. "I guess so, Mr. Myers," he said.

"It's iron, Dad," Moonic said, laughing. "It's never been glass!"

MATT CHRISTOPHER ®

THE #1 SPORTS SERIES FOR KIDS

Read them all!

- Baseball Turnaround
- The Basket Counts
- Body Check
- Catch That Pass!
- Catcher with a Glass Arm
- Comeback of the Home Run Kid
- Dirt Bike Racer
- Dirt Bike Runaway
- Football Double Threat
- Football Nightmare
- Goalkeeper in Charge
- The Great Quarterback Switch
- Halfback Attack*
- The Hockey Machine
- The Home Run Kid Races On
- Hook Shot Hero
- Hot Shot
- Ice Magic
- Johnny Long Legs
- Karate Kick
- The Kid Who Only Hit Homers

- Lacrosse Firestorm
- Long-Arm Quarterback
- Long Shot for Paul
- The Lucky Baseball Bat
- Miracle at the Plate
- Out at Second
- Power Pitcher**
- QB Blitz
- Return of the Home Run Kid
- Skateboard Renegade
- Skateboard Tough
- Slam Dunk
- Snowboard Champ
- Snowboard Maverick
- Soccer Duel
- Soccer Hero
- Soccer Scoop
- Spike It!
- Stealing Home
- The Submarine Pitch
- Tough to Tackle

All available in paperback from Little, Brown and Company
* Previously published as Crackerjack Halfback
** Previously published as Baseball Pals

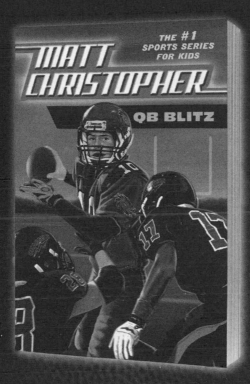
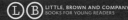

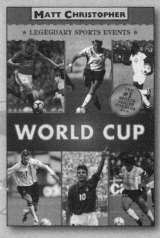
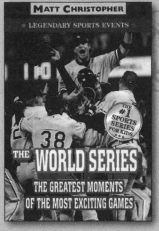
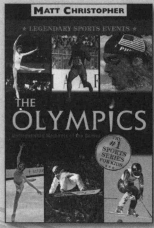